TWIST COTTAGE

To Patrick Jepher.

The sharpest man in London.

Orchard Books
338 Euston Road, London NW1 3BH
Orchard Books Australia
Hachette Children's Books
Level 17/207 Kent Street, Sydney, NSW 2000

First published by Orchard Books in 1999 or 2000
This edition published in 2008
Text copyright © Anthony Horowitz 1999

The right of Anthony Horowitz to be identified
as the author of this work has been asserted by him
in accordance with the Copyright, Designs and Patents Act, 1988.

A CIP catalogue record for this book is available from the British Library

ISBN 978 1 84616 973 1

7 9 10 8

www.hachette.co.uk

Printed and bound in Great Britain by CPI Bookmarque, Croydon, CR0 4TD

Orchard Books is a division of Hachette Children's Books,
an Hachette UK company.

About the Author

Anthony Horowitz was brought up on horror stories, and his childhood love of all things sinister and scary has stayed with him. The stories in this book are inspired by ordinary, everyday objects and events, as are most of the stories in the rest of the series. But each of them has a twist to remind us that even in a safe, predictable world, the horrible and unexpected, the blood-curdling and the spine-chilling, are never far away.

Anthony Horowitz is the highly successful author of a bestselling range of books, including detective stories, adventure stories and spy stories which have been translated into over a dozen languages. He is also a well-known television screenwriter with credits including *Poirot*, *Midsomer Murders* and *Foyle's War*. Anthony lives in East London.

'A first class children's novelist'
TIMES EDUCATIONAL SUPPLEMENT

'Perfect for readers with an appetite for ghoulish happenings'
SCHOOL LIBRARIAN ASSOCIATION

'Suspenseful and exciting'
BOOKS FOR KEEPS

A N T H O N Y
HOROWITZ

TWIST COTTAGE

ORCHARD BOOKS

<u>Contents</u>

TWIST
cottage
9

harriet's
HORRIBLE
dream 45

TWIST
cottage

I never knew my mother.

She died in a car accident the year after I was born and I was brought up, all on my own, by my dad. I had no brothers and no sisters. There were just the two of us, living in a house in Bath which is down in the South-West, in Avon. My dad worked as a history lecturer at Bristol University and for ten years we had nannies or housekeepers living with us, looking after me. But by the time I was thirteen and going to a local school, we found we didn't really need anyone any more, so there were just the two of us. And we were happy.

My dad's name is Andrew Taylor. He never talked about my mother but I think he must have loved her a lot because he didn't remarry and (although he doesn't like me to know it) he kept a photograph of her in his wallet and never went anywhere without it. He was a big, shaggy man with glasses and untidy brown hair that had just started to go grey. His clothes always looked old, even when they were brand new, and they never fitted him very well. He was forty-five. He went to the cinema a lot. He listened to classical music. And, like me, he supported Arsenal.

The two of us always got on well, perhaps because we always had our own space. We only had a small house in Bath – it was in one of the back streets behind the antique market – but we both had our own rooms. Dad had a small study on the ground floor and, when I was ten, he converted the attic into a play area for me. It was a little cramped with a slanting roof and only one small window but it was fine for me; somewhere private where I could go. In fact we didn't see much of each other during the week. He was at university and I was at school. But at weekends we went to films together, did the shopping, watched TV or kicked a football around...all the things that every father does with every son. Only there was no mother to share it.

We were happy. But everything changed with the coming of Louise. I suppose it had to happen in the end. My dad might be middle-aged but he was still fit and reasonably good-looking. I knew he went out with women now and then. But until Louise, none of them had ever stayed.

She was a few years younger than him. She was a mature student at Bristol University. She was studying art but she had taken history as an option and that was how they met. The first time I met her, she'd come round to the house to pick up a book and I have to say I could see what my dad saw in her. She was a very beautiful woman, tall and slim, with dark hair, brown eyes and a very slight French accent (her mother lived in Paris). She was smartly dressed in a silk dress that showed off her figure perfectly. The one thing that was strange though was that, for a student, she didn't seem particularly interested in either history or art. When my dad talked about some gallery he'd been to she was soon yawning (although she was careful to hide it behind a handkerchief) and whenever he asked her about her work she quickly changed the conversation to something else. Even so, she stayed for tea and insisted on doing the washing-up. My dad didn't say anything after she'd gone but I could see that he was taken by her. He stood in the doorway for a long time, watching her leave.

I began to see more and more of Louise. Suddenly there were three of us going to the cinema, not two. Three of us having lunch together at the weekend. And inevitably, there she was one morning when I came down to breakfast. I was old enough not to be shocked or upset that she'd stayed the night. But it was still a shock. I was happy for him but secretly sad for myself. And…well, for some reason, she worried me too.

My dad and I spoke about her only once. 'Tell me something, Ben,' he said, one day. We were out walking, following the canal path as it wove through Bath Valley. It was something we often liked to do. 'What do you think of Louise?'

'I don't know,' I said. In a way she was perfect but maybe that was what worried me. She was almost too good to be true.

'You know, there's never been anyone since your

mother died,' he said. He stopped and looked up at the sky. It was a lovely day. The sun was shining brilliantly. 'But sometimes I wonder if I ought to be on my own. After all, you're almost fourteen. Any day now you'll be leaving home. What would you say if Louise and I were to...'

'Dad, I just want you to be happy,' I interrupted. The conversation made me feel uncomfortable. And what else could I say?

'Yes.' He smiled at me. 'Thank you, Ben. You're a good boy. You'd have made your mother proud...'

And so they got married at Bath Registry Office. I was the best man and I made a speech at the lunch afterwards, tied a plastic dog poo to the car and threw confetti at them as they drove away. They had a week's honeymoon in Majorca and even that should have rung a slight alarm bell because my dad had told me that he'd really wanted to visit some of the historical towns in the South of France. But Louise had her own way and they must have had a good time because when they got back they were happy and relaxed with deep suntans and a load of presents for me.

I suppose the marriage was a success for about three months but it all went wrong very quickly after that.

Although she agreed to come with us when we visited the new Tate gallery in Millbank, Louise suddenly gave up her art course. She said it bored her, and anyway, she wanted to spend more time looking after my dad. This sounded all right at the time and she may even have meant what she said. But the house got messier and messier. It was true that Dad and I had never been exactly tidy. Mrs Jones, our old cleaner, was always complaining about us. But we never left dirty mugs in the bedroom, tangled hair in the sink or crumpled clothes on the stairs. Louise did and when Mrs Jones complained one Tuesday morning, there was a nasty row and the next thing I knew was that Mrs Jones had resigned. Louise didn't do any more cooking after that. All the food she ever prepared seemed to have come out of tins or out of the freezer and as my dad was a bit of a health freak, mealtimes were always a disappointment.

Of course, neither of us had expected Louise to cook and clean for us. That wasn't the idea. My dad was really sorry she'd decided to give up her course at the university. The trouble was that she didn't seem to want to fit in and the slightest argument always ended with her flying into a rage with slamming doors and tears. At heart she was a bit of a spoiled child. She always had to have her own way. Shortly after she moved in, she suddenly insisted that Dad let her have my attic room because she wanted somewhere to paint. Dad came to me very reluctantly and asked me if I'd mind and I didn't argue because I knew it would lead to another row and I didn't want him to be unhappy. So that was how I lost my room.

Dad was unhappy though and as the first year shuddered slowly by, I could see that he was getting worse and worse. He lost weight. The last traces of brown faded out of his hair. He never laughed any more. Louise had told him that his clothes were old-fashioned and made him look middle-aged and one day she had given the whole lot to a charity shop.

Now my dad wore jeans and T-shirts that didn't suit him and actually made him look older than he had before. He wasn't allowed to play classical music any more either. Louise preferred jazz and most of the time the house was filled with the wail of trumpets and clarinets, fighting with the constant drone of the television which she never seemed to turn off. And although she had loaded a few canvases and paints into my old room, she never actually produced anything.

My dad never complained about her. I suppose this was part of his character. If I'd been married to her, I'd have probably walked out by now, but he seemed to accept everything meekly. However, one afternoon towards the end of the summer, we found ourselves retracing our steps along the canal and, perhaps remembering our conversation from the year before, he turned to me and suddenly said, 'I'm afraid Louise isn't a very good mother to you.'

I shrugged. I didn't know what to say.

'Perhaps it would have been better if I'd stayed single.' He sighed and fell silent. 'Louise has asked me to sell the house,' he suddenly blurted out.

'Why?'

'She says it's poky. She says she doesn't like living in the town. She wants me to move more into the countryside.'

'You're not going to, are you, Dad?'

'I don't know. I'm thinking about it...'

He sounded so sad. And it should have been obvious to him, really. The marriage wasn't working, so why not divorce her? I almost said as much but perhaps it was as well that I didn't. For things came to a head that very night and I realised just how poisonous Louise could be.

The two of them argued quite often. At least, Louise did. Generally, my dad preferred to suffer in silence. But that night my dad got his bank statement. It seemed that Louise had bought herself a whole load of designer clothes and stuff like that. She'd spent almost a thousand pounds. He didn't shout at her but he did criticise her. And suddenly she was screaming at him. I heard the whole thing from my bedroom. It was impossible not to.

'I know you don't love me,' she cried in a whiny, petulant voice. 'You and Ben have been against me from the day I arrived.'

'I really don't think things are working out,' my dad said, quietly.

'You want me to go? Is that it? You want a divorce?'

'Perhaps we might both be happier...'

'Oh no, Andrew. If you want to divorce me, it's going to cost you. I want half of everything you have. And I'm entitled to it! You'll have to move out of this house – and that's just for a start. I'll tell the social workers how you've always left Ben on his own when he gets back from school. That's not allowed. So they'll take him away and you'll never see him again.'

'Louise...'

'I'll tell the university how cruel you've been to me. I'll tell them you battered me and you'll lose your job. I'll take your money. I'll take your son. I'll take everything! You wait and see!'

'Please, Louise...there's no need for this.'

After that, things quietened down. Louise knew she

had my dad round her little finger and every day she found new ways to be cruel to him. I think she only asked him to move to upset him. She knew how happy we'd always been in that little house.

As always she had her way. About three months after the argument, my dad said he'd found somewhere.

The somewhere was a little house called Twist Cottage.

If Louise wanted to move into the countryside, she couldn't have chosen a better house than Twist Cottage, although it wasn't actually her who had chosen it. Dad found it. He came home one day with the details and we went to see it that same afternoon.

Twist Cottage was buried in the middle of a wood not far from the aqueduct where the Avon Canal and the River Avon cross paths. It's a strange part of the world. There are small towns scattered all over the place but walk a few metres into the woods and you seem to tumble into the middle of nowhere. Twist

Cottage was as isolated as a cottage can be. It seemed to be imprisoned by the trees that surrounded it, as if they were afraid of its being found. And yet it was a very pretty building, straight out of a jigsaw puzzle with a thatched roof, black beams and windows made of diamond-shaped pieces of glass. The cottage was as twisted as its name suggested. My dad said it was very old, Elizabethan or earlier, and time had worn all the edges into curves. It had a big garden with a pond in the middle. The grass was already long.

'We'll need a mower,' Louise said.

'Yes,' my father agreed.

'And I'm not doing the mowing!'

Now I don't know a lot about house prices but I do know that Avon is an expensive place to live, mainly because of all the Londoners who've bought second homes there. But the strange thing was that my dad bought Twist Cottage for only a hundred thousand pounds which isn't very much at all. Not in Avon. I wondered about that at the time. I also noticed that the estate agent – a Mr Willoughby – seemed particularly happy to have sold it. He had an office in Bath and the day he sold Twist Cottage, he gave everybody the day off.

As it happened, one of my best mates at school was a boy called John Graham and his older sister, Carol, was Mr Willoughby's secretary. I was around at their house the week after the sale had been agreed and she told me about the day off. In fact she told me a lot more.

'You're not really moving into Twist Cottage, are you?' she demanded. She was nineteen years old, with frizzy hair and glasses. She had a slightly turned up nose which suited her attitude to life. 'Poor you!'

'What are you talking about?' I asked.

'Mr Willoughby never thought we'd sell it.'

'Is there something wrong with it?'

'You could say that.' Carol had been painting her nails with scarlet polish. She closed the bottle and came over to me. 'It's haunted,' she said.

'Haunted?'

'Mr Willoughby says it's very haunted. He says it's the most haunted house he's ever known.'

John and I both burst out laughing.

'It's true!'

'Do you believe in ghosts?' John asked his sister.

'I don't believe in ghosts,' I said.

'Well there's something wrong with the house,' Carol insisted. 'Why else do you think your dad got it so cheap?'

She probably wouldn't have bothered talking to us, but she had nothing to do while her nails dried. So that was how I found out the recent history of Twist Cottage. And it wasn't very nice.

Over the last few years, six different couples had moved into the place and something horrible had happened to every one of them. A lady called Mrs Webster was the first.

'She drowned in the bath,' Carol said. 'Nobody knew how it happened. It wasn't as if she was old or anything like that. When they found her, she was all bloated. She'd completely swollen up inside!'

That was the first time Willoughby sold the house. It was bought by a second couple, a Mr and Mrs Johnson from London. Just four weeks later, one of them had fallen out of the window and got impaled on the garden fence.

The next victim was a Dr Stainer. Carol knew all the names. She was enjoying telling us her story, sitting in the living room of her house as the sun set and long shadows reached across the room. 'This time it was a tile falling off the roof,' she said. 'Dr Stainer's skull was fractured and death was instantaneous.

'After that, the house was empty for about six months. Word had got around, you see. All these deaths. But eventually Mr Willoughby sold it again. I forget who bought it this time. But I do know that whoever it was had a heart attack just two weeks later and the house had to be sold for a fifth time.

'It was bought by a Professor Bell. The professor lasted just one month before falling down the stairs.'

'Also killed?' John demanded.

'Yes. With a broken neck – and the house went back on the market once again. Poor Mr Willoughby never thought he'd be rid of it. He didn't even want to handle it. But of course he was making money every time it was sold, even though the price was dropping and dropping. Who would want to live in a house where so many people had died?'

'Was my dad the next one to buy it?' I asked.

'No. There was one more owner before your dad. An Australian. Electrocuted while adjusting the thermostat on the deep freeze.'

There was a long silence. Either Carol had been talking for longer than I thought or the sun had set more rapidly than usual because it was suddenly quite dark.

'You're not really moving in there, are you, Ben?' John asked.

'I don't know,' I replied. All of a sudden I wasn't feeling too good. 'Is this all true, Carol? Or are you just trying to scare me?'

'You can ask Mr Willoughby,' Carol said. 'In fact you can ask anyone. Everyone knows about Twist Cottage. And everyone knows you'd be mad to live there!'

That night I asked my dad if he knew what he was getting himself into. Louise was already asleep. She'd started drinking recently and had got through half a bottle of malt whisky before dragging herself upstairs and throwing herself into bed. Dad and I talked in whispers but we didn't need to. She was sound asleep. You could probably hear her snoring on the other side of Bath.

'Is it true, Dad?' I asked. 'Is Twist Cottage haunted?'

He looked at me curiously. For a moment I thought I saw a flicker of anger in his eyes. 'Who have you been talking to, Ben?' he demanded.

'I was at John's house.'

'John? Oh…his sister.' My dad paused. He was looking very tired these days. And old. It made me feel sad. 'You don't believe in ghosts, do you?' he asked.

'No. Not really.'

'Nor do I. For heaven's sake, Ben, this is the twenty-first century!'

'But Carol said that six people died there in just two years. There was an Australian, a Professor Bell, a doctor…'

'It's too late now!' my dad interrupted. He never raised his voice as a rule but this time he was almost shouting. 'We're moving there!' He forced himself to calm down. 'Louise likes the house and she'll only be disappointed if I change my mind.' He reached out and tousled my hair like he used to, when I was younger, before Louise came. 'You don't have anything to worry about, Ben, I promise you,' he said. 'You'll be happy there. We all will.'

And so we moved in. I'd tried to forget what Carol had told me, but I have to admit I was still feeling a bit uneasy and things weren't helped by two accidents that happened the very day we arrived. First of all the driver of the removal van tripped and broke an ankle. I suppose it could have happened anywhere and it wasn't as if a ghost had suddenly popped up and gone 'boo' or something like that but still it made me think. And then, at the end of the day, a carpenter who had been called in to mend a broken window frame slipped with a saw and nearly cut off a finger. There was a lot of blood. It formed something that looked almost like a question mark on the window-pane. But what was the question?

Why have we come here?

Or – *What's going to happen next?*

In fact nothing happened for a while. The next weeks were mainly spent unpacking boxes. There were piles everywhere – books, plates, clothes, CDs – and no matter how many boxes we unpacked there always seemed to be more waiting to be done. A new dishwasher was delivered and also a mower big enough to deal with the garden, a great beast of a thing that Dad had found second-hand and which only just fitted into the shed. Louise didn't help with anything. I couldn't help noticing that recently she had become very plump. Perhaps it was all the drinking. She liked to sleep in the afternoon and shouted at us if we woke her up.

Of course, I was out most afternoons. My dad had bought me a new bike, partly to cheer me up, but mainly because I now needed it to get to school. There was a bus I could catch into Bath from the nearby town of Bradford-on-Avon but that was still a ten-minute cycle ride away. In fact I preferred to cycle the whole way, following the canal towpath where dad and I had often walked. It was a beautiful ride when the weather was good and this was the summer term – warm and sunny. I'd leave the bus until the weather got cold.

Twist Cottage had three bedrooms. Mine was at the back of the house with views into the wood. Well, all the rooms looked into the wood as we were completely surrounded. It was a small room with uneven, white walls that bulged slightly inwards, and a curiously ugly wooden beam that ran along the ceiling just above the window. Once my bed was in and my Arsenal posters were on the wall, I suppose it was cosy enough, but in a way it was creepy too. All those trees cast shadows. There were shadows everywhere and when the wind blew and the branches waved the whole room was filled with flickering, dancing shapes.

And there was something else. Maybe I was just imagining it, but the cottage always felt colder than it had any right to be. Even in the middle of the summer there was a sort of dampness in the air. I could feel it creeping over my shoulders when I got out of the bath. It was always there, slithering round the back of my neck. When I got into bed I would bury myself completely under the duvet but even then it would still find a way to twist itself round my ankles and tickle my toes.

Dad was right, though. Louise did seem happier in Twist Cottage. She wasn't doing anything very much any more. All her art stuff seemed to have got lost in the move and she spent most of the day in bed. She was getting fatter and fatter. I often used to see her sitting with a magazine and a box of chocolates with the TV on and the curtains closed. My poor dad had to do everything for her; the shopping, the cooking, the laundry…as well as his job at the university. But at least she didn't shout at him so much any more. She was like a queen, happy so long as she was being served.

And then the incident happened that very nearly removed Louise from our life for ever. I was there and I saw what happened. Otherwise I would never have believed it.

It was a Saturday, another warm day at the end of

August. Dad was in Bristol. I was at home mending a puncture on my bike. Louise hadn't got up until about eleven o'clock and after her usual three bowls of cornflakes and five slices of toast, she had decided to step out into the garden. This was in itself a rare event but, like I say, it was a lovely day.

Anyway, I saw her waddle down to the fishpond. She had a tub of fish food in her hand. Maybe her own enormous breakfast had reminded her that the fish hadn't actually been fed since we moved in. She stopped at the side of the water and tipped some of the flakes into her hand.

'Here! Fishy fishies!' she called out. She still had a little girl voice.

Something moved in the grass behind her. She didn't see it, but I did. At first I thought it was a snake. A long, green snake with some sort of orange head. But there are no huge, green snakes in Avon. I looked again. That was when I saw what it was and, like I say, if somebody had described it to me I wouldn't have believed them, but I was there and I saw it with my own eyes.

It was the garden hose. Moving on its own.

I was sitting there with a bicycle chain in one hand and oil all the way up to my elbows. I watched the hose slither and twist through the long grass while Louise stood at the edge of the water scattering a fistful of food across the surface. I opened my mouth to call out but no words came.

And then the hose looped itself around her ankles and tightened. Louise yelled out, losing her balance. Her hand jerked back, sending fish food flying in an arc behind her. She toppled forward and there was a tremendous splash as she hit the water. It must have surprised the fish.

The fish pond was deep and covered in slimy green algae. Despite the weather, the water was freezing. I have no doubt at all that if I hadn't been there, Louise would have died. It took me a few seconds to recover from the surprise but of course I dropped the bike chain and ran down to help her. No. That's not completely true. I didn't go straight away. I hesitated. And a horrible thought flashed through my mind.

Leave her to drown. Why not? She's ruined Dad's life. She's made us sell our old house. She's cruel and she's lazy and she's always complaining. We'll be better off without her.

That's what I thought. But an instant later I was on my feet and running. I wouldn't have been able to live with myself if I'd done anything else. I got to the edge of the pond and reached out for her. I caught hold of her dress and pulled her towards me. She was filthy and sobbing, her yellow hair matted with dark green weeds. I managed to get her out on to the grass and she sat there, a great lump, water streaming down her body. And did she thank me?

'I suppose you think that's funny!' she moaned.

'No,' I said.

'Yes you do! I can see it!' She wiped a hand across her face. 'I hate you. You're a spiteful, horrible boy.' And with that she stomped off into the house.

The hose pipe lay where it was.

That evening, I told my dad what had happened. Louise had gone back to bed after the accident (if that's the right word). She'd also locked the bedroom door so he couldn't have gone in if he'd wanted to. I told him first that she'd fallen into the pond and I described how I'd saved her. Then I told him about the hose. But even as I explained what I'd seen, I saw his face change. I'd expected him to be incredulous, not to believe me. But it was more than that. He was angry.

'The hose moved,' he said, repeating what I'd said. The three words came out slowly, heavily.

'I saw it, Dad.'

'Was it the wind?'

'No. There was no wind. It's exactly like I saw. It sort of...came alive.'

'Ben, do you really expect me to believe that? Are you saying it was magic or something? Fairies? I mean, for heaven's sake, you're fourteen years old. Hoses don't come alive and move on their own...'

'I'm only telling you what I saw.'

'You're telling me what you thought you saw. If I didn't know you better I'd say you'd been sniffing glue or something.'

'Dad – I saved her life!'

'Yes. Well done.'

He walked out of the house and I didn't see him

again that evening. It was only later, when I was lying in bed, that I realised what had really upset him. It wasn't a pleasant thought but I couldn't escape it.

Maybe he would have been happier if I had done what I was tempted to do. Maybe he would have preferred it if I'd left Louise to drown.

My story is almost over…and this is where I have to admit that I actually missed the climax. That happened about a week later and I was away for the weekend. Perhaps it's just as well, because what happened was really horrible.

Louise got minced.

She had been lying in the garden sunbathing and somehow the mowing machine, the one I've mentioned, turned itself on. It rumbled out of the shed and across the lawn and towards her. She was lying on a towel, listening to music through headphones. That's why she didn't hear it coming. I can imagine her last moments. A shadow must have fallen across her eyes. She would have looked up just in time to see this great, metallic monster plunging on to her, the engine roaring, the blades spinning, diesel smoke belching out thick and black. When the police arrived, Louise was a mess. Parts of her had hit the wall twenty metres away.

Whenever a wife is killed in unusual circumstances – and circumstances couldn't have been more unusual than these – the police always suspect the husband. Fortunately, my dad was in the clear. At the time Louise had died, he had been lecturing to two hundred students. As for me, I was in London, so obviously I had nothing to do with it either. There was an inquest, a month after the death, and we all had to go to court and listen to police reports and witness statements. The lawn mower had been taken apart and examined and there was a report about that. But in the end, there could only be one verdict. Accidental death. And that was the end of that.

Except it wasn't.

We never went back to Twist Cottage. I was glad about that. I thought of all the deaths that had taken place there over the years...and now Louise! It could have been me or my dad next.

We moved into rented accommodation in Bath and my dad took time off from university to sort everything out. I wasn't sure what would happen to us, where we would live and stuff like that. But now it turned out that we were actually very rich. It seemed an incredible coincidence but just before we had moved into Twist Cottage, Dad had taken out an insurance policy on Louise's life. If she died as a result of an accident or an illness, my dad would receive three quarters of a million pounds! Of course, the insurance company was suspicious. They always are. But the police had investigated. There had been an inquest. There was nothing they could do except pay.

And so we were able to buy a new house in Bath, just round the corner from the one we had sold. We tried to put Louise behind us. Everything began to go back to the way it had been before.

And then, one day, I happened to find myself at Bristol University. I'd arranged to meet Dad when he finished work. We were going to the cinema together – just like the old days. Only he'd got held up in a tutorial or something and I found myself kicking my heels in the little square box that he called his study.

There was a desk with a photograph of me (but not one of Louise, I noticed) and a scattering of papers. There were a couple of chairs and a sofa. Two of the walls were lined with shelves and there were books everywhere. I think there must have been a thousand books in the room. They were even piled up on the floor, half-covering the window.

I figured I'd read something while I was waiting but of course they were all history books. Then I noticed a *Viz* comic on one of the shelves and I reached up for that but somehow my fingers caught one of the books which had been lying flat, out of sight. It slid out and toppled into my arms. I found myself looking at the cover. It was called *Haunted Houses from the Elizabethan Age*.

I was curious. It was almost as if my dad had hidden the book right up on the highest shelf, as if he didn't want it to be seen. I carried it over to the desk and opened it.

And there it was, on the first page, among the chapter headings.

Twist Cottage.

I sat down and this is what I read.

One of the most famous witches of the sixteenth century was Joan Barringer who lived in a cottage in the woods near Avoncliffe. Unlike many of the witches, who were usually elderly spinsters, Joan Barringer was married. Her husband, James Barringer, was a blacksmith. Sometime around the year 1584, in the twenty-seventh year of the reign of Queen Elizabeth, James Barringer began an affair with a local girl, Rose Edlyn, daughter of Richard Edlyn, a wealthy landowner.

It seems that somehow Joan Barringer found out about the affair. Her revenge was swift and terrible. She placed a curse on the unfortunate girl and in the weeks that followed, Rose Edlyn became ill. She lost weight.

She lost her hair. She went blind. Finally, she died. The recently-discovered letters written by Richard Edlyn show what happened next.

James Barringer was persuaded to testify against his wife. She was summoned to court on a charge of witchcraft and sentenced to death. The method of execution was to be burning at the stake. However, before the sentence could be carried out, she managed to escape from prison and returned to her cottage in Avoncliffe. The house was surrounded. The local villagers were determined that the evil woman should pay the price for what she had done.

And it was then that Joan Barringer made her appearance. Standing at an upstairs window, with a rope draped around her neck, she screamed out a final curse. Any woman who ever entered Twist Cottage would die. She blamed women for what had happened to her. Rose Edlyn had been beautiful and had stolen her husband from her. She had been ugly and would die unloved.

Then she jumped. The rope was tied to a beam. It broke her neck and she ended up dangling in front of the villagers, her head wrenched to one side. The last letter written by Richard Edlyn reads:

'...and so we did discover that wretched, evil crone, a sight most horrible to behold. Her eyes were swolne and bloodie. Her fanges were drawne. And so she hung by her twysted neck beside that horrid, twysted house.'

This is how Twist Cottage got its name.

So Dad had known about the history of Twist Cottage before we moved in. That was my first thought. But there was more to it than that. I remembered how angry he had become when I had asked him if it was haunted.

'For heaven's sake, Ben, this is the twenty-first century...'

That's what he'd said. But he'd known.

He'd known that the house had been cursed – and that the curse only worked on women! Could it possibly be true? I used the telephone in his office and called Carol, the girl who had warned me about Twist Cottage in the first place. Six people had died there, she had told me. And now she confirmed what I already knew. Mrs Webster had drowned in the bath.

Mrs Johnson had fallen out of a window. Dr Stainer had fractured her skull and Professor Bell had fallen down the stairs. Both of them had been women. Another woman had had a heart attack and an Australian woman had electrocuted herself.

I thought back to the day we had moved in. The driver who had broken an ankle and the carpenter who had slipped with a saw. Both of them had been women too.

My head was spinning. I didn't want to think about it. But there could be no avoiding the truth. Louise had ruined my dad's life and had refused to give him a divorce. All along he must have wanted to kill her but he couldn't do it himself. So he had moved her into Twist Cottage – knowing that, since we were both male, he and I would be safe – and had waited for the ghost of Joan Barringer to do the job for him.

It was incredible!

I put the book back on the shelf and left the room.

I never, ever asked him about it. In fact we never mentioned Twist Cottage again.

But there is one other thing to mention.

My dad hung on to Twist Cottage. He didn't sell it. With all the money he got from the insurance, he didn't need to. But later on I found out that he rented it out from time to time. He demanded an awful lot of money, but the men who rented it always paid.

It was always men. They would go with their cruel, nagging wives. Or their screeching, senile grandmothers. One took his mother. Another went with a peculiarly vindictive aunt.

The women only stayed there a short time.

None of them ever came back.

harriet's
HORRIBLE
dream

What
made
the dream
so horrible
was that
it was
so *vivid*.

Harriet actually felt that she was sitting in a cinema, rather than lying in bed, watching a film about herself. And although she had once read that people only ever dream in black-and-white, her dream was in full Technicolor. She could see herself wearing her favourite pink dress and there were red bows in her hair. Not, of course, that Harriet would have *dreamt* of having a black and white dream. Only the best was good enough for her.

Nonetheless, this was one dream that she wished she wasn't having. Even as she lay there with her legs curled up and her arms tight against her sides, she wished that she could wake up and call for Fifi – her French nanny – to go and make the breakfast. This dream, which could have gone on for seconds but at the same time seemed to have stretched through the whole night, was a particularly horrid one. In fact it was more of a nightmare. That was the truth.

It began so beautifully. There was Harriet in her pink dress, skipping up the path of their lovely house just outside Bath, in Wiltshire. She could actually hear herself singing. She was on her way back from school, and a particularly good day it had been too. She had come top in spelling and even though she knew she had cheated – peeking at the words which she had hidden in her pencil case – she had still enjoyed going to the front of the class to receive her merit mark. Naturally, Jane Wilson (who had come second) had said some nasty things but Harriet had got her own back, 'accidentally' spilling a glass of milk over the other girl during lunch.

She was glad to be home. Harriet's house was a huge, white building – nobody in the school had a bigger house than her – set in a perfect garden complete with its own stream and miniature waterfall. Her brand-new bicycle was leaning against the wall outside the front door although perhaps she should have put it in the garage as it had been left out in the rain for a week now and had already begun to rust. Well, that was Fifi's fault. If the nanny had put it away for her, it would be all right now. Harriet thought about complaining to her mother. She had a special face for when things went wrong and a way of squeezing out buckets of tears. If she complained hard enough, perhaps Mummy would sack Fifi. That would be fun. Harriet had already managed to get four nannies sacked. The last one had only been there three weeks!

She opened the front door and it was then that things began to go wrong. Somehow she knew it even before she realised what was happening. But of course that was something that was often the case in dreams. Events happened so quickly that you were aware of them before they actually arrived.

Her father was home from work early. Harriet had already seen his Porsche parked in the drive. Guy Hubbard ran an antiques shop in Bath although he had recently started dabbling in other businesses too. There was a property he was developing in Bristol, and something to do with time-share apartments in Majorca. But antiques were his main love. He would tour the country visiting houses, often where people had recently died. He would introduce himself to the widows and take a look around, picking out the treasures with a practised eye. 'That's a nice table,' he would say. 'I could give you fifty pounds for that. Cash in hand. No questions asked. What do you say?' And later on that same table would turn up in his shop with a price tag for five hundred or even five thousand pounds. This was the secret of Guy's success. The people he dealt with never had any idea how much their property was worth. But he did. He once said he could smell a valuable piece even before he saw it.

Right now he was in the front living room, talking to his wife in a low, unhappy voice. Something had gone wrong. Terribly wrong. Harriet went over to the door and put her ear against the wood.

'We're finished,' Guy was saying. 'Done for. We've gone belly-up, my love. And there's nothing we can do.'

'Have you lost it all?' his wife was saying. Hilda

Hubbard had once been a hairdresser but it had been years since she had worked. Even so, she was always complaining that she was tired and took at least six holidays a year.

'The whole bloody lot. It's this development. Jack and Barry have cleared out. Skipped the country. They've taken all the money and they've left me with all the debts.'

'But what are we going to do?'

'Sell up and start again, old girl. We can do it. But the house is going to have to go. And the cars...'

'What about Harriet?'

'She'll have to move out of that fancy school for a start. It's going to be a state school from now on. And that cruise the two of you were going on. You're going to have to forget about that!'

Harriet had heard enough. She pushed open the door and marched into the room. Already her cheeks had gone bright red and she had pressed her lips together so tightly that they were pushing out, kissing the air.

'What's happened?' she exclaimed in a shrill voice.

'What are you saying, Daddy? Why can't I go on the cruise?'

Guy looked at his daughter unhappily. 'Were you listening outside?' he demanded.

Hilda was sitting in a chair, holding a glass of whisky. 'Don't bully her, Guy,' she said.

'Tell me! Tell me! Tell me!' Harriet had drawn herself up as if she was about to burst into tears. But she had already decided she wasn't going to cry. On the other hand, she might try one of her ear-splitting screams.

Guy Hubbard was standing beside the fireplace. He was a short man with black, slicked back hair and a small moustache. He was wearing a checked suit with a red handkerchief poking out of the top pocket. He and Harriet had never really been close. In fact, Harriet spoke to him as little as possible and usually only to ask him for money.

'You might as well know,' he said. 'I've just gone bankrupt.'

'What?' Harriet felt the tears pricking her eyes despite herself.

'Don't be upset, my precious baby doll…' Hilda began.

'*Do* be upset!' Guy interrupted. 'There are going to be a few changes around here, my girl. I can tell you that. You can forget your fancy clothes and your French nannies...'

'Fifi?'

'I fired her this morning.'

'But I liked her!' The tears began to roll down Harriet's cheeks.

'You're going to have to start pulling your weight. By the time I've paid off all the debts we won't have enough money to pay for a tin of beans. You'll have to get a job. How old are you now? Fourteen?'

'I'm twelve!'

'Well you can still get a paper round or something. And Hilda, you're going to have to go back to hair. Cut and blow dry at thirty quid a time.' Guy took out a cigarette and lit it, blowing blue smoke into the air. 'We'll buy a house in Bletchley or somewhere. One bedroom is all we can afford.'

'So where will I sleep?' Harriet quavered.

'You can sleep in the bath.'

And that was what did it. The tears were pouring

now – not just out of Harriet's eyes but also, more revoltingly, out of her nose. At the same time she let out one of her loudest, shrillest screams. 'I won't! I won't! I won't!' she yelled. 'I'm not leaving this house and I'm not sleeping in the bath. This is all your fault, Daddy. I hate you and I've always hated you and I hate Mummy too and I am going on my cruise and if you stop me I'll report you to the NSPCC and the police and I'll tell everyone that you steal things from old ladies and you never pay any tax and you'll go to prison and see if I care!'

Harriet was screaming so loudly that she had almost suffocated herself. She stopped and sucked in a great breath of air, then turned on her heel and flounced out of the room, slamming the door behind her. Even as she went, she heard her father mutter, 'We're going to have to do something about that girl.'

But then she was gone.

And then, as is so often the way in dreams, it was the next day, or perhaps the day after, and she was sitting at the breakfast table with her mother who was eating a bowl of low-fat muesli and reading the *Sun* when her father came into the kitchen.

'Good morning,' he said.

Harriet ignored him.

'All right,' Guy said. 'I've listened to what you had to say and I've talked things over with your mother and it does seem that we're going to have to come to a new arrangement.'

Harriet helped herself to a third crumpet and smothered it in butter. She was being very prim and lady-like, she thought. Very grown up. The effect was only spoiled when melted butter dribbled down her chin.

'We're moving,' Guy went on. 'But you're right. There isn't going to be room for you in the new set-up. You're too much of a little miss.'

'Guy…' Hilda muttered, disapprovingly.

Her husband ignored her. 'I've spoken to your Uncle Algernon,' he said. 'He's agreed to take you.'

'I don't have an Uncle Algernon,' Harriet sniffed.

'He's not really your uncle. But he's an old friend of the family. He runs a restaurant in London. The

'Sawney Bean'. That's what it's called.'

'That's a stupid name for a restaurant,' Harriet said.

'Stupid or not, it's made a bomb. He's raking it in. And he needs a young girl like you. Don't ask me what for! Anyway, I've telephoned him today and he's driving down to pick you up. You can go with him. And maybe one day when we've sorted ourselves out...'

'I'll miss my little Harry-Warry!' Hilda moaned.

'You won't miss her at all! You've been too busy playing bridge and having your toes manicured to look after her properly. Maybe that's why she's turned into such a spoilt little so-and-so. But it's too late now. He'll be here soon. You'd better go and pack a bag.'

'My baby!' This time it was Hilda who began to cry, her tears dripping into her muesli.

'I'll take two bags,' Harriet said. 'And you'd better give me some pocket money too. Six months in advance!'

Uncle Algernon turned up at midday. After what her father had said, Harriet had expected him to drive a Rolls-Royce or at the very least a Jaguar and was disappointed by her first sight of him, rattling up the drive in a rather battered white van with the restaurant name, SAWNEY BEAN, written in blood-red letters on the side.

The van stopped and a figure got out, almost impossibly, from the front seat. He was so tall that Harriet was unsure how he had ever managed to fit inside. As he straightened up, he was much taller than the van itself, his bald head higher even than the aerial on the roof. He was also revoltingly thin. It was as if a normal human being had been put on a rack and stretched. His legs and his arms, hanging loose by his side, seemed to be made of elastic. His face was unusually repulsive. Although he had no hair on his head, he had big, bushy eyebrows which didn't quite fit over his small, glistening eyes. His skin was the colour of a ping-pong ball. His whole head was roughly the same shape. He was wearing a black coat with a fur collar round his neck and gleaming black shoes which squeaked when he walked.

Guy Hubbard was the first one out to greet him.

'Hello, Archie!' he exclaimed. The two men shook hands. 'How's business?'

'Busy. Very busy.' Algernon had a soft, low voice that reminded Harriet of an undertaker. 'I can't hang around, Guy. I have to be back in town by lunch. Lunch!' He licked his lips with a wet, pink tongue. 'Fully booked today. And tomorrow. And all week. Sawney Bean has been more successful than I would ever have imagined.'

'Coining it in, I bet.'

'You could say that.'

'So have you got it then?'

Algernon smiled and reached into the pocket of his coat, pulling out a crumpled brown envelope which he handed to Guy. Harriet watched, puzzled, from the front door. She knew what brown envelopes meant when her father was concerned. This man, Algernon, was obviously giving him money – and lots of it from the size of the envelope. But he was the one who was taking her away to look after her. So shouldn't Guy have been paying *him*?

Guy pocketed the money.

'So where is she?' Algernon asked.

'Harriet!' Guy called.

Harriet picked up her two suitcases and stepped out of the house for the last time. 'I'm here,' she said. 'But I hope you're not expecting me to travel in that perfectly horrid little van…'

Guy scowled. But it seemed that Algernon hadn't heard her. He was staring at her with something in his eyes that was hard to define. He was certainly pleased by what he saw. He was happy. But there was something else. Hunger? Harriet could almost feel the eyes running up and down her body.

She put the cases down and grimaced as he ran a finger along the side of her face. 'Oh yes,' he breathed. 'She's perfect. First class. She'll do very well.'

'What will I do very well?' Harriet demanded.

'None of your business,' Guy replied.

Meanwhile, Hilda had come out on to the drive. She was trembling and, Harriet noticed, refused to look at the new arrival.

'It's time to go,' Guy said.

Algernon smiled at Harriet. He had dreadful teeth.

They were yellow and uneven and – worse – strangely pointy. They were more like the teeth of an animal. 'Get in,' he said. 'It's a long drive.'

Hilda broke out in fresh tears. 'Aren't you going to kiss me goodbye?' she wailed.

'No,' Harriet replied.

'Goodbye,' Guy said. He wanted to get this over with as soon as possible.

Harriet climbed into the van while Algernon placed her cases in the back. The front seat was covered in cheap plastic and it was torn in places, the stuffing oozing through. There was also a mess on the floor; sweet wrappers, old invoices and an empty cigarette pack. She tried to lower the window but the handle wouldn't turn.

'Goodbye, Mummy! Goodbye, Dad!' she called through the glass. 'I never liked it here and I'm not sorry I'm going. Maybe I'll see you again when I'm grown up.'

'I doubt it...' Had her father really said that? That was certainly what it sounded like. Harriet turned her head away in contempt.

Algernon had climbed in next to her. He had to coil his whole body up to fit in and his head still touched the roof. He started the engine up and a moment later the van was driving away. Harriet didn't look back. She didn't want her parents to think she was going to miss them.

The two of them didn't speak until they had reached the M4 motorway and begun the long journey east towards the city. Harriet had looked for the radio, hoping to listen to music. But it had been stolen, the broken wires hanging out of the dashboard. She was aware of Algernon examining her out of the corner of his eye even as he drove and when this became too irritating she finally spoke.

'So tell me about this restaurant of yours,' she said.

'What do you want to know?' Algernon asked.

'I don't know…'

'It's very exclusive,' Algernon began. 'In fact it's so exclusive that very few people know about it. Even so, it is full every night. We never advertise but word gets around. You could say that it's word of mouth. Yes. Word of mouth is very much what we're about.'

There was something creepy about the way he said that. Once again his tongue slid over his lips. He smiled to himself, as if at some secret joke.

'Is it an expensive restaurant?' Harriet asked.

'Oh yes. It is the most expensive restaurant in London. Do you know how much dinner for two at my restaurant would cost you?'

Harriet shrugged.

'Five hundred pounds. And that's not including the wine.'

'That's crazy!' Harriet scowled. 'Nobody would pay that much for a dinner for two.'

'My clients are more than happy to pay. You see…' Algernon smiled again. His eyes never left the road. 'There are people who make lots of money in their lives. Film stars and writers. Investment bankers and businessmen. They have millions and millions of pounds and they have to spend it on something. These people think nothing of spending a hundred pounds on a few spoonfuls of caviar. They'll spend a thousand pounds on a single bottle of wine! They go to all the smartest restaurants and they don't care how much they pay as long as their meal is cooked by a famous cook, ideally with the menu written in French and all the ingredients flown, at huge expense, from all around the world. Are you with me, my dear?'

'Don't call me "my dear",' Harriet said.

Algernon chuckled softly. 'But of course there comes a time,' he went on, 'when they've eaten everything there is to be had. The best smoked salmon and the finest fillet steak. There are only so many ingredients in the world, my dear, and soon they find they've tasted them all. Oh yes, there are a thousand ways to prepare them. Pigeon's breast with marmalade and foie gras. Smoked sea bass with shallots and Shitaki mushrooms. But there comes a time when they feel they've had it all. When their appetites become jaded. When they're looking for a completely different eating experience. And that's when they come to Sawney Bean.'

'Why did you give the restaurant such a stupid name?' Harriet asked.

'It's named after a real person,' Algernon replied.

He didn't seem ruffled at all even though Harriet had been purposefully trying to annoy him. 'Sawney Bean lived in Scotland at the start of the century. He had unusual tastes...'

'I hope you're not expecting me to work in this restaurant.'

'To work?' Algernon smiled. 'Oh no. But I do expect you to appear in it. In fact, I'm planning to introduce you at dinner tonight...'

The dream shifted forward and suddenly they were in London, making their way down the King's Road, in Chelsea. And there was the restaurant! Harriet saw a small, white-bricked building with the name written in red letters above the door. The restaurant had no window and there was no menu on display. In fact, if Algernon hadn't pointed it out she wouldn't have noticed it at all. He indicated and the van turned into a narrow alley, running behind the building.

'Is this where you live?' Harriet asked. 'Is this where I'm going to live?'

'For the next few hours,' Algernon replied. He pulled

up at the end of the alley in a small courtyard surrounded on all sides by high brick walls. There was a row of dustbins and a single door, sheet metal with several locks. 'Here we are,' he said.

Harriet got out of the van and as she did so the door opened and a short, fat man came out, dressed entirely in white. The man seemed to be Japanese. He had pale orange skin and slanting eyes. There was a chef's hat balanced on his head. When he smiled, three gold teeth glinted in the afternoon light.

'You got her!' he exclaimed. He had a strong oriental accent.

'Yes. This is Harriet.' Algernon had once again unfolded himself from the van.

'Do you know how much she weigh?' the chef asked.

'I haven't weighed her yet.'

The chef ran his eyes over her. Harriet was beginning to feel more and more uneasy. The way the man was examining her...well, she could almost have been a piece of meat. 'She very good,' he murmured.

'Young and spoilt,' Algernon replied. He gestured

at the door. 'This way, my dear.'

'What about my cases?'

'You won't need those.'

Harriet was nervous now. She wasn't sure why but it was not knowing that made her feel all the worse. Perhaps it was the name. Sawney Bean. Now that she thought about it, she *did* know it. She'd heard that name on a television programme or perhaps she'd read it in a book. Certainly she knew it. But how...?

She allowed the two men to lead her into the restaurant and flinched as the solid metal door swung shut behind her. She found herself in a gleaming kitchen, all white-tiled surfaces, industrial-sized cookers and gleaming pots and pans. The restaurant was closed. It was about three o'clock in the afternoon. Lunch was over. It was still some time until dinner.

She became aware that Algernon and the chef were staring at her silently, both with the same excited, hungry eyes. Sawney Bean! *Where* had she heard the name?

'She perfect,' the chef said.

'That's what I thought,' Algernon agreed.

'A bit fatty perhaps…'

'I'm not fat!' Harriet exclaimed. 'Anyway, I've decided I don't like it here. I want to go home. You can take me straight back.'

Algernon laughed softly. 'It's too late for that,' he said. 'Much too late. I've paid a great deal of money for you, my dear. And I told you, we want you here for dinner tonight.'

'Maybe we start by poaching her in white wine,' the chef said. 'Then later tonight with a Béarnaise sauce…'

And that was when Harriet remembered. Sawney Bean. She had read about him in a book of horror stories.

Sawney Bean.

The cannibal.

She opened her mouth to scream but no sound came out. Of course, it's impossible to scream when you're having a bad dream. You try to scream but your mouth won't obey you. Nothing will come out. That was what was happening to Harriet. She could feel the scream welling up inside her. She could see Algernon and the chef closing in on her. The room was spinning, the pots and pans dancing around her head, and still the scream wouldn't come. And then she was sucked into a vortex and the last thing she remembered was a hand reaching out to support her so she wouldn't bruise herself, wouldn't damage her flesh when she fell.

Mercifully, that was when she woke up.

It had all been a horrible dream.

Harriet opened her eyes slowly. It was the most delicious moment of her life, to know that everything that had happened *hadn't* happened. Her father hadn't gone bankrupt. Her parents hadn't sold her to some creep in a white van. Fifi would still be there to help her get dressed and serve up the breakfast. She would get up and go to school and in a few weeks' time she and her mother would leave on their Caribbean cruise. She was annoyed that such a ridiculous dream should have frightened her so much. On the other hand, it had seemed so realistic.

She lifted a hand to rub her forehead.

Or tried to.

Her hands were tied behind her. Harriet opened her eyes wide. She was lying on a marble slab in a kitchen. A huge pot of water was boiling on a stove. A Japanese chef was chopping onions with a glinting stainless steel knife.

Harriet opened her mouth.

This time she was able to scream.

Enter the strange and twisted
world of Anthony Horowitz –
                    if you dare!

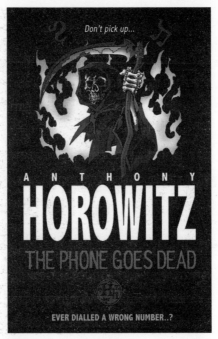

Don't pick up...

A N T H O N Y

HOROWITZ

THE PHONE GOES DEAD

EVER DIALLED A WRONG NUMBER..?

ISBN 978 1 84616 972 4   £3.99

Two twisted tales to curdle your blood.

David's mobile won't stop ringing, but these are no ordinary callers. He seems to have a hotline to heaven...or hell.

Isabel has a nasty feeling that the Victorian bath her parents have installed is *waiting* for her. But it won't be a bubble bath she gets, more of a bloodbath.

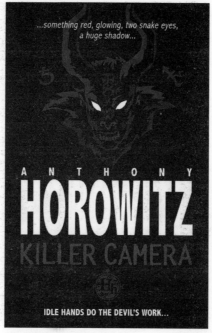

ISBN 978 1 84616 971 7   £3.99

Two spine-chilling stories guaranteed to keep you awake at night.

Jamie is pleased with the camera he finds at a car boot sale, until he realises that everything he photographs breaks...or dies.

Henry soon finds that his new computer has a life of its own, and it's not afraid to gamble – with people's lives!

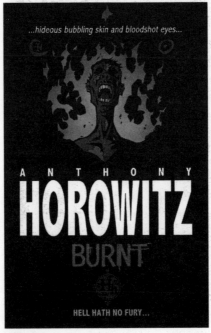

ISBN 978 1 84616 966 3   £3.99

Three ~~Two~~ creepy stories to send shivers down your spine.

Uncle Nigel is determined to get a sun tan. But Tim is sure there's something sinister going on as his uncle's skin starts to frazzle and his brain begins to fry.

When Bart buys a magical monkey's ear in a market in Marrakesh, he discovers that making wishes is a dangerous game.

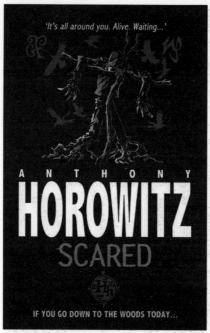

'It's all around you. Alive. Waiting...'

A N T H O N Y
HOROWITZ
SCARED

IF YOU GO DOWN TO THE WOODS TODAY...

ISBN 978 1 84616 968 7   £3.99

Three sinister stories to fill you with fear.

Gary hates the countryside. It's boring. But something has got it in for Gary. Perhaps the countryside hates him too?

Kevin loves computer games, but this latest one breaks all the rules, and it's ruthless....

Howard's in heaven...so why does it feel more like hell?

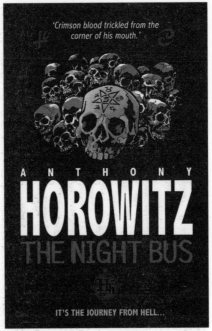

'Crimson blood trickled from the corner of his mouth.'

ANTHONY
HOROWITZ
THE NIGHT BUS

IT'S THE JOURNEY FROM HELL...

ISBN 978 1 84616 967 0   £3.99

Three terrifying tales you'll wish you'd never read.

It's Halloween but the living dead on the night bus home aren't trick-or-treaters!

When his dad picks up a hitchhiker, Jacob finds himself in a life-or-death situation. Someone is harbouring a deadly secret.

And who is the man with the yellow face in Peter's passport photo – because it isn't him, is it?

ISBN 978 1 84616 973 1   £3.99

Two spooky stories guaranteed
to give you nightmares.

All the previous owners of Twist Cottage have died suddenly. Surely a coincidence, thinks Ben. But is it?

Harriet is having a horrible dream, but any minute now she'll wake up and it will all be OK...won't it?

ISBN 978 1 84616 969 4   £5.99

Evil is waiting…

It's a world where everything seems normal…but the weird, the sinister and the truly terrifying are lurking just out of sight. Like an ordinary camera…with evil powers; a bus ride home that turns into your worst nightmare; and a mysterious computer game that nobody would play, if they knew the rules. Each story has a shocking sting in its tale…

ISBN 978 1 84616 970 0   £5.99

Abandon hope...

It's a world where everything seems normal...but the spooky, the shocking and the positively petrifying are lurking just out of sight. Like a hitchhiker...who isn't quite all he seems; a scary cottage with a grisly secret; and a mobile phone...that let's you contact the dead. Each story has a shocking sting in its tale...

More Orchard Black Apples

❏ The Phone Goes Dead	*Anthony Horowitz*	978 1 84616 972 4	£3.99
❏ Killer Camera	*Anthony Horowitz*	978 1 84616 971 7	£3.99
❏ Burnt	*Anthony Horowitz*	978 1 84616 966 3	£3.99
❏ Scared	*Anthony Horowitz*	978 1 84616 968 7	£3.99
❏ The Night Bus	*Anthony Horowitz*	978 1 84616 967 0	£3.99
❏ Twist Cottage	*Anthony Horowitz*	978 1 84616 973 1	£3.99
❏ Little Soldier	*Bernard Ashley*	978 1 86039 879 7	£4.99
❏ Revenge House	*Bernard Ashley*	978 1 84121 814 4	£4.99
❏ The Snog Log	*Michael Coleman*	978 1 84121 161 9	£4.99
❏ The Drop	*Anthony Masters*	978 1 84362 196 6	£4.99

Orchard Black Apples are available from all good bookshops,
or can be ordered direct from the publisher:
Orchard Books, PO BOX 29, Douglas IM99 1BQ
Credit card orders please telephone 01624 836000
or fax 01624 837033 or visit our website:
www.orchardbooks.co.uk
or e-mail: bookshop@enterprise.net for details.

To order please quote title, author and ISBN
and your full name and address.
Cheques and postal orders should be made payable to 'Bookpost plc.'
Postage and packing is FREE within the UK
(overseas customers should add £2.00 per book).

Prices and availability are subject to change.